WALT DISNEY

PICTURES PRESENTS

THE

Tigger

MOVIE

The Onliest Tigger

Walt Disney Pictures Presents THE Tigger MOVIE

The Onliest Tigger

Adaptation by Leslie Goldman

Disney PRESS

New York

WALT DISNEY
PICTURES PRESENTS
THE
Tigger
MOVIE

The Onliest Tigger

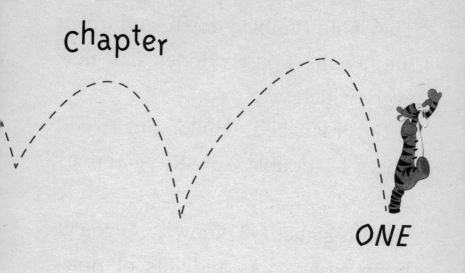

It was a blustery morning in the Hundred-Acre Wood. Winter was near. And as usual, Tigger felt like bouncing.

Tigger sprang up high . . . and landed . . . right on Winnie the Pooh.

They both tumbled down, and rolled into Pooh's house. Honey jars flew every which way.

Tigger laughed. "Hullo! I'm Tigger! That's T-I—double-Guh—Rrr, and that's me!"

Pooh sighed. "I know . . . you've bounced me lots and lots of times before."

Tigger stood up. One of his feet landed in a sticky pot of honey. He tried to shake it off. "Yeah, fun, ain't it? Sayyy . . . speakin' o' which, ya wanna go bouncin' with me? On accounta bouncing is what tiggers do . . . um . . . best!"

Pooh began to straighten his over-turned honeypots. He looked at the pot on Tigger's foot and shook his head. "Well, I would go bouncing with you, Tigger. Except that I must count all these honeypots to be sure that I have enough for winter."

Tigger kicked and kicked, but he couldn't get the pot loose.

"Let me get that, please," said Pooh. He took hold of the pot and tugged. Suddenly Tigger's foot popped out. Pooh tumbled back-ward, scattering his pots all over again! One pot landed—*Kerplop!*—on Pooh's head.

Tigger cleaned his foot. "Yeach!" he yelled. "What do Pooh Bears like about this icky sticky stuff, anyway? Well, no time for goofing off," he added. "I've got dawdling to do. So, T-T-F-N, Ta-Ta-for-Now!"

Tigger bounced off, leaving Pooh happily humming with his head stuck in his honeypot.

chapter

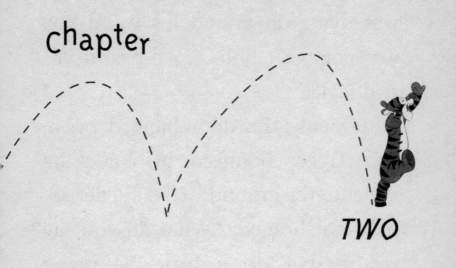

TWO

Tigger bounced to Piglet's house next.

Piglet was trying to stay warm inside his cold, cold house. He hugged himself and stood beside his little fireplace with his teeth chattering. But his fire was dying down and his wood box was empty. "Ohhh . . . d-dear-dear," said Piglet.

Suddenly the door banged open, and Tigger bounced in, knocking Piglet to the ground. "Hiya, Piglet, ol' pal!" he shouted. "What do you say you and I do a little bouncing together! Hoo-*hoo*!"

"B-b-b-b-b-b-b-bouncing? Oh my," chattered Piglet. He pointed to his fireplace. "You see, Tigger, I haven't enough firewood to last the winter and . . ."

"Why, sure ya do!" interrupted Tigger. "There's lots of firewood lying all over the place!" Tigger picked up one of Piglet's wooden chairs and threw it in the fireplace. "There! See? Nice and warm!"

"Well, it is . . . warm . . . but I would really rather prefer that my firewood not have quite so much . . . chair . . . in it," said Piglet.

Tigger shrugged. "Suit yourself! As for me, I've got bouncing to do! T-T-F-N!"

Tigger bounced away into the forest, until he reached Kanga and Roo's house. Kanga was sweeping the leaves in front of her house.

"Hoo-hoo-hoo-*hoo*!" Tigger cried

out. "Why, hullo there and good mornin', Mrs. Kanga, ma'am!"

"Well, good morning, Tigger dear," replied Kanga.

"She called me dear," Tigger said to himself, then he added, to Kanga, "Pardon me for askin', but you wouldn't happen to be interested in doin' a bit of bouncin' with me, would ya?"

Just then Roo, who had been inside the house, looked outside and saw Tigger. Roo gasped excitedly. He loved to bounce with Tigger.

But Tigger didn't see Roo. He only heard Kanga say that she was too busy to go bouncing with him.

So by the time Roo raced outside to play with his friend, Tigger had already bounced off into the woods.

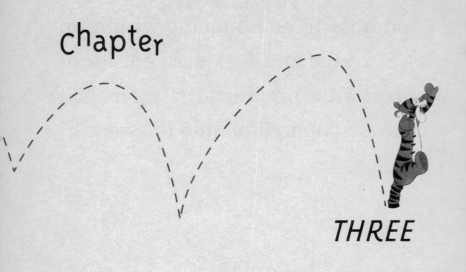

THREE

Tigger bounced through the forest alone, trying to make sense of the situation. He jumped up on top of a giant boulder to think. "I wonder why nobody wants to bounce with me?"

Tigger listened for an answer, but none came. "Oh well, heh," he said with a shrug. "There's plenty of others I haven't asked yet!" He jumped off the boulder. His jump jiggled the boulder and started it rolling downhill.

It rolled and rolled, picking up speed, until—*CRASH*—it landed right on top of Eeyore's house, smashing it into toothpicks!

Eeyore's friends rushed over as soon as they heard what had happened. They all gathered around and looked at the boulder and at Eeyore's house *under* the boulder.

"We need a contraption to move this boulder. I'll draw up the plans," Rabbit said.

So Rabbit designed and built an amazing rock-moving contraption. But there was just one problem. No matter how hard everyone tried, they couldn't make the contraption work. As they pushed and tugged and pulled and shoved, Tigger bounced up.

"All this boulder needs is a little bouncing!" he exclaimed.

And before Rabbit could stop him, Tigger bounced a huge bounce. With a noise like a giant rubber band breaking, the contraption broke loose and flew into the air, taking everyone with it.

Tigger bounced down to where his friends had landed. They were picking themselves up out of briar patches and mud puddles, treetops and creek beds.

"Now does anyone want to go bouncing with me?" he asked.

"Just look at this mess," Rabbit scolded. "Everything's ruined, and all you can think about is bouncing."

"But that's what tiggers do best!" Tigger said.

"But—we're not tiggers," Pooh answered sadly.

"You mean nobody wants to bounce with me?" asked a stunned and sad Tigger.

Everyone was silent. And finally, Tigger slowly turned and walked away.

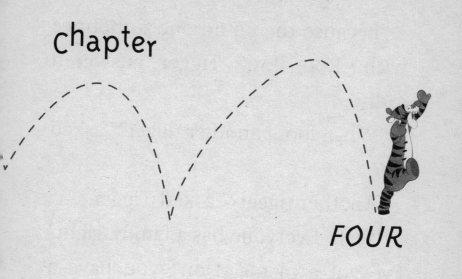

"**W**ho needs them other fellas, anyhow?" said Tigger, sniffling to himself.

Roo followed Tigger. "Don't be sad, Tigger," he said. "Why don't you go bouncing? That'll cheer you up."

"Because there's no one to bounce with, Roo Boy," Tigger answered sadly.

"What about another tigger?" asked Roo.

"Another tigger?" asked Tigger.

"Yeah. Everyone has a family, right? I've got a mama. Don't you have a family somewhere, too?" asked Roo.

"Why that's ridicu . . . I mean, er . . . a family fulla tiggers, ya say . . . heh, heh, can you imagine such a thing!" Tigger liked the idea so much, he began to leap and dance. "Why, there'd be more tiggers than ya can stick a shake at! And we'd all be bouncing! Bouncing morning, noon, and nighty-night!"

But how would Tigger find his family?

"I know, let's ask Owl," Roo suggested. "He'll know what to do."

So Tigger and Roo hurried to Owl's tree house.

"My dear boy," said Owl. "If I may go out on a limb here, I would first and foremost suggest that to find one's family, one must first look up one's family tree."

"My family tree?" asked Tigger. "Why didn't I think of that? So long, Beak Lips. Thanks for the tip! Hoo-hoo-hoo-*hoo*!"

Off he and Roo went, in search of his family tree.

"Tigger, how are you gonna know which tree is your family tree?" asked Roo.

"Why that's obvious, Roo Boy! My tigger family tree has gotta be the biggest, hugest, and most gigantical tree in all the entire Hundred-Acre Woodses, on account of all the enormous numerous numbers of tigger family members that'll be on it! And besides and furthermore, it'll be all stripedy, just like yours truly!"

Tigger and Roo bounced by Pooh, Piglet, Rabbit, and Eeyore, who were just finishing building a new house for Eeyore.

"Hiya, Donkey Boy!" shouted Tigger.

"Oh! It's you, Tigger and Roo!" said Piglet.

"Back to his bouncy old self," said Eeyore.

Tigger examined a tree near Eeyore's house. "Is this perhaps a tigger family tree up there?" he asked. "Hallooooo! Tigger family? Hallooo?" he shouted, bouncing to the next tree and the next and the next.

Piglet, Pooh, Rabbit, and Eeyore

watched until Tigger and Roo were out of sight.

"Pooh Bear, I didn't know that Tigger had a f-f-family," said Piglet.

"Neither did I, Piglet," said Pooh. "Only . . . it appears that he has lost them."

"Seems to be looking for them," said Eeyore.

"Was that something that w-we were supposed to be doing too?" asked Piglet.

"Why I believe it must be, Piglet. I quite often forget to remember these sorts of things. Come on," said Pooh.

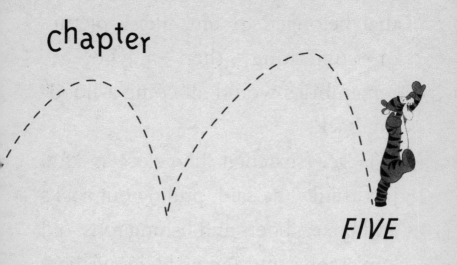

chapter

FIVE

After a long day of searching, Tigger and Roo walked home. "Just where aren't those tiggers, anyway?" asked Tigger. "What I need to do is find some sorta clue to their where-abouts. If I found some thingamabob that belonged to 'em, like a picture or something, then maybe the remembries would all come a-flooding back!"

Tigger searched his closets. "An' just think," he said, pulling out socks and boxes, boots and fishing rods, old apple cores and tennis balls, "if there are other tiggers, we could all bounce the Whoop-de-Dooper Loop-de-Looper Alley-Ooper Bounce!"

"If you could teach me the Whoopy Super Dooper Bounce, then I could bounce just like you," said Roo.

"Teach ya the Whoop-de-Dooper

Bounce? That's ridickerous! It's a very powerful bounce and it's only for professional bouncers," said Tigger.

"But I'm a really good bouncer!" said Roo. "I could do the Whoopie-Doopie . . . uh, the Looper-Duper . . . uh, if you'd teach me!" said Roo.

"Well, all right," said Tigger. "Firs' ya swing yer legs up high . . . and ya twist yer tail in tight! Wind up all yer springs . . . and with yer eyes fixated straight ahead . . . ya let it all loose!"

Roo took a deep breath and wound himself tighter and tighter. He tied his body in knots. He crouched down . . . wound up . . . and bounced—off the walls, off the ceiling—and right into Tigger's closet! *Crash! Crumple! Bang! Thud!* Stuff came pouring out. Roo staggered out with things tangled all over him—including a shiny, heart-shaped locket.

"Roo!" Tigger shouted. "You've found the exact thingamabob I was looking for! And it must have a picture of my tigger family inside it!"

"Oh boy!" said Roo.

Tigger tried to open the lid, but it wouldn't budge. He shook it and pounded on it, and even used a can opener. Finally, he pried it open with a sword. But as Tigger and Roo looked inside, their faces fell.

"It's kinda . . . sorta . . ." began Roo.

"Empty. Completely tiggerless," sighed Tigger. "How am I supposed to find my family now?"

As Tigger slumped unhappily at his desk, Roo noticed a stack of paper, envelopes, and stamps.

"Maybe there's another way to reach your family," Roo said. He handed Tigger a pen. "Why don't you write them a letter?"

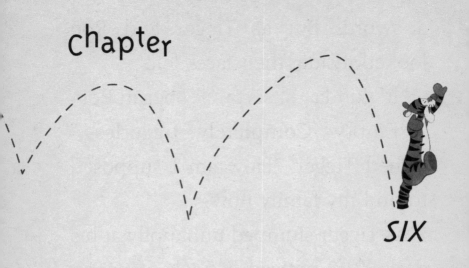

Tigger sat down at his desk and began to write.

"Dear T-I–double-Guh–Rrrs, Tiggers. Greetings and salivatins. Please drop by any ol' time, on accounta my house is yer house and versa vicey. Love, Tigger."

26

Tiggers love to bounce!

Rabbit builds an amazing rock-moving contraption.

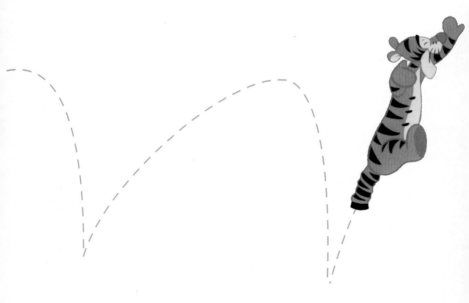

"Everything's ruined, and all you can think about is bouncing!" Rabbit scolds.

"My dear boy," says Owl. "To find one's family, one must first look up one's family tree."

"My tigger family tree has gotta be the biggest, hugest, and most gigantical tree in the Hundred-Acre Woodses!"

"Now there's nothing to do but wait."

Tigger gets ready for his family reunion.

"My very own one-and-only family!"

Tigger's friends decide to go in search of Tigger.

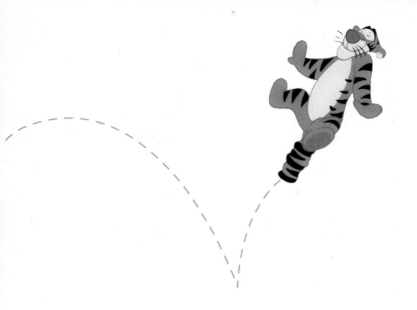

They get caught in a blinding blizzard!

"Tigger's family?" says Christopher Robin. "Why Tigger, you didn't have to go looking for them."

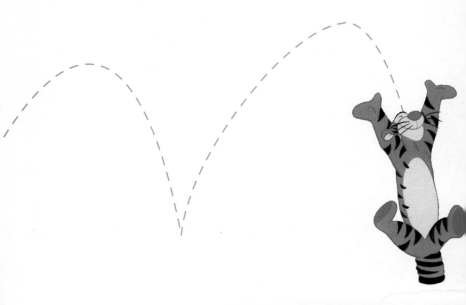

"There! That ought to do it!" he said. He raced out to the mailbox and dropped it in. "Hoo-hoo-hoo-*hoo*! Now there's nothing ta do but wait!" With Roo by his side, Tigger leaned up against the mailbox and waited. They waited, and waited.

It started to snow, and still Tigger and Roo waited. It got dark, and they were still waiting.

"I gotta go home now," Roo said finally. "Mama will be worried about me."

Tigger sighed. "Aw, why am I kidding myself? They're not coming." He began to sniffle. "Because I may as well face it. There aren't any other tiggers." He looked at the empty locket around his neck. "And I guess that means this silly old thing's gonna stay empty for all of forever."

"But isn't that a wonderful thing about tiggers? Being the only one?" tried Roo.

"You betcha, Roo Boy!" Tigger shuffled toward his house, trying to sing. "Oh, the most wonderful thing about tiggers is . . . I'm the very onli-est one."

Sadly, Roo went home. Later that night, just before bedtime, he practiced his bouncing.

"Whatever are you doing, Roo, dear?" asked Kanga.

"I'm practicing the Whoopdie Doopie Bounce. Maybe if I could do it really good for Tigger, he wouldn't miss not having a family so much. But . . . I can't bounce it yet," said Roo.

"Well, I'm sure you'll be able to do it in time, dear," said Kanga.

"But Tigger seems awful lonely, don't you think, Mama?" asked Roo.

"I suppose he might be, every now and again," she answered.

"Mama?" said Roo.

"Yes, dear?"

"I wish I had a big brother like Tigger," said Roo.

"Now, why wish that, when you have a Tigger like Tigger?" said Kanga.

"Because then I'd be his little brother. And he'd be just like one of our family. Wouldn't that be great?" asked Roo.

"But, Roo, dear, Tigger is just like one of our family," said Kanga. "And as long as we care for him . . . he always will be."

"I just wish I could do something to make him feel better," said Roo.

chapter

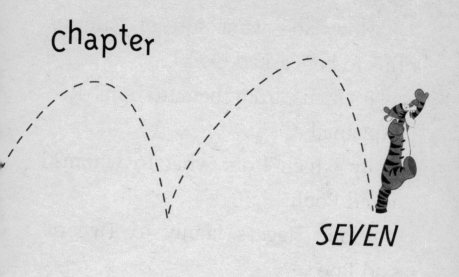

SEVEN

The next day, Roo had an idea. He and the others would write Tigger a letter, as if it was from his own tigger family. Roo gathered everyone together at Owl's house to explain his plan.

"Now, ah—what sort of letter is this to be?" asked Owl.

"It's by us, from them, to him," Roo explained.

"By which from what to whom?" asked Pooh.

"From Tigger's family to Tigger!" said Roo.

Owl picked up his pen and began to write. "Dear Tigger. Just a note to say . . . well, what shall I say?" he asked.

"Well, I suppose it might say . . . Dress warmly," said Kanga.

"Oh, I see! Excellent advice!" said Owl, bending over the letter to write.

"Oh, Owl," said Pooh. "Perhaps
. . . Eat well?"

"Good point, Pooh Bear," said Owl.

"Stay s-safe . . . and sound," said
Piglet.

"A very good idea, Piglet," said
Pooh.

"Keep smiling," said Eeyore.

"We're always there for you!" said
Roo.

"Wishing you all the best. Signed,
Your Family," finished Owl.

chapter

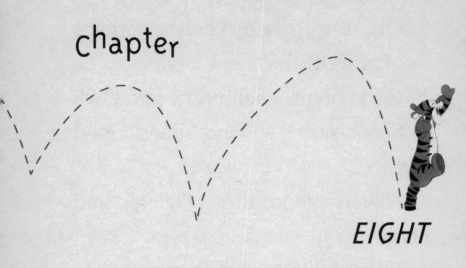

EIGHT

Early the next morning, the Hundred-Acre Wood rang with Tigger's happy shouts as he bounced through the forest, calling his friends.

"Pooh Boy! Hoo-hoo-*hoo*! Pigleeeeet!" he bellowed. "Kaaaanga! Roooo! Eeyore!

Eeyore, old buddy! Lookit what I got! A letter! A letter for me, that's who! T-I—double-Guh—Rrr spells Tigger!" he said.

"I wonder who it might be from," said Piglet.

"From my very own family! I knew I had one," said Tigger. "They miss me something awful and they're coming to see me . . . tomorrow!" Tigger said.

"Tomorrow?" gulped Roo.

"Now, where does it say that, exactly?" asked Owl.

"Exackatackly nowhere, cause with us tiggers you gotta read betwixt the lines!" said Tigger. He jumped up with glee. "I'm gonna see my whole family, 'cause my whole family is all coming to see little old you know who-hoo-hoo!"

"Oh, the most wonderful thing about tiggers is . . . I'm not the only one!" sang Tigger.

Tigger rushed home to get ready for his family reunion. He built a family room addition to his house. He cleaned. He decorated. He baked.

And while he was doing all that, his friends worried. What would happen to Tigger when no family members showed up?

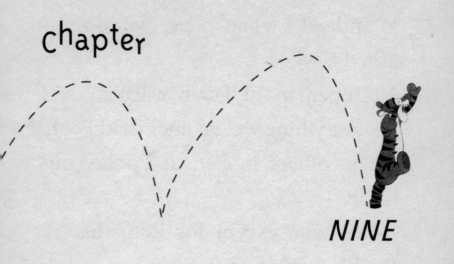

chapter

NINE

"**S**omeone should try to tell him that we wrote the letter," Roo said. But Tigger was so excited, no one had the heart to tell him the truth.

"Oh, the poor dear . . . he'll be so disappointed," said Kanga.

"Indeed, what have we done?" asked Owl.

"Or perhaps his family will come and . . . everything will be fine?" said Pooh.

The others looked at Pooh, confused.

Everyone except for Roo, that is. Pooh's words gave him an idea. "That's it!" he exclaimed. "We'll all dress up like tiggers!"

In a few hours, Kanga's house was full of tiggers. Poohish tiggers, Owlish tiggers, even an Eeyorish tigger. Everyone had on masks and baggy suits and lots and lots of painted black drippy stripes.

"What we have to do is act really tiggery," Roo explained. "We gotta do a lot of bouncing, and say a lot of tigger stuff."

"Aha! Such as . . . Hoo. Hoo. Hoo. Whoooo!" said Owl.

"Abso . . . p-p-p-p-posilutely?" said Piglet.

"And T-T-F . . . G? Or is it T-T-F what?" tried Pooh.

"Well, that's kinda sorta like Tigger," said Roo.

Suddenly Rabbit burst into the room. "Thank goodness I found you all here! There's a terrible storm headed for . . ." Rabbit stopped and stared at his friends with his mouth open.

"What on earth are you doing?" he yelled. "Stripes? Have you lost your minds? You should be covering the windows, counting your supplies, gathering firewood! Winter is here and—and you aren't even ready!"

Rabbit's words made everyone stop and think a moment. Perhaps he was right, after all.

"Well, I really don't have enough f-f-firewood," said Piglet.

"And I am down to this last lonely honeypot," said Pooh.

"Come to think of it, we don't really

look or act very much like tiggers," said Owl.

"I thought I was pretty convincing," said Eeyore.

"Wait, wait," said Roo. "We have to do it. We have to! Think how sad Tigger's gonna feel."

"We don't really know how to be tiggers," said Pooh.

"But if we're all happy," said Roo, "he's sure to realize that we're his family."

And so the gang went to Tigger's house.

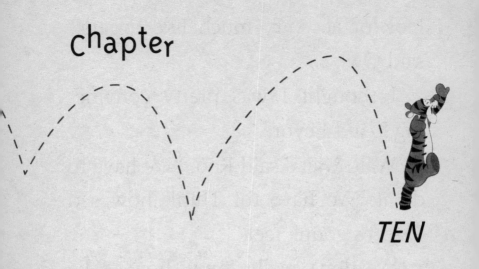

TEN

When Tigger heard a knock at his door, he jumped up. "Hold on, tiggers! I'm coming to get ya!" he shouted.

He opened the door to see his friends—dressed in funny tigger outfits. "Is it . . . is it . . . is it really you, my very own one and only family!" he shouted. "Come on in! There's lotsa catchin' uppin' we gotta do! We haven't seen each other in—we haven't seen each other! Heh heh . . . heh heh . . ."

"Gee, it's nice to have all us tiggers getting together like this!" said Roo, nervously.

The others nodded. But no one could think of what to say next.

"So, what ya been up to, cousin?" Tigger asked Piglet at last.

"I've b-b-b-been . . . um, uh," said Piglet.

"Bouncing! Bouncing morning, noon, and nighty-night!" finished Roo.

"Why, that's what I've been doing, too!" said Tigger. "I know! Let's all do what tiggers do best. That would be bouncing, of course."

"Of course!" Tigger's friends shouted. "Absoposilutely! Bouncing's what tiggers do best!"

So everyone began to bounce. They had a wonderful time.

Roo was so happy that his plan was working so well. Then he had another idea. "Wait a second! We gotta bounce the Whoop-de-Dooper Loop-de-Looper Alley-Ooper Bounce!" he said.

"What a Tiggerific idea! Hoo-hoo-hoo-*hoo*!" shouted Tigger. "Guests first."

Roo warmed up. "Ya gotta swing yer legs up high . . . and twist yer tail in tight . . . wind up all yer springs . . . and with yer eyes fixated straight ahead . . ." he shouted. "Ya let it all loose with a hoo-hoo-hoo-*HOOOOOO*!" He bounced, right into the closet. Everything came pouring out. And his tigger disguise fell off!

"Roo, what are you doing impersonating a tigger?" Tigger asked. He pulled the masks off all his friends. "Piglet? Owl? Kanga? Eeyore? What are you doing?"

"We only wanted to help, Tigger," said Pooh.

"Oh, now I understand. It was all a big joke," said Tigger. He stomped to his dresser drawer and pulled out his locket. "Well, that's all right. Some-where out there, there's a tigger family tree full of my real tigger family! I got a letter to prove it. And I'm gonna find them!" He left, slamming the door behind him.

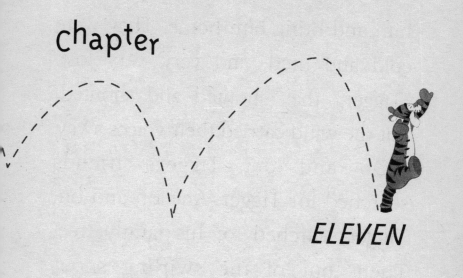

chapter

ELEVEN

As the cold winds blew strong and hard, and the snow fell, Tigger trudged through the woods searching for his family.

Back home, his friends worried about him. So off they went to find him and bring him home. They were cold and tired, and very, very lost. "Tigger," they shouted and shouted, but the wind carried their voices away.

On and on, Tigger's friends searched for Tigger. And on and on, Tigger searched for his family tree. Then, out of the swirling snow, Tigger saw an enormous tree. "My family tree," he shouted. "I found it! I found it!" He dashed for the tree and scrambled into the branches looking for his family.

Not far away, Roo and the others heard Tigger's shouts and rushed to meet him, calling his name.

When Tigger heard their voices, he leaped from the tree. "Hoo-hoo-hoo-*hoo*!" he shouted. "Looks like the whole family's here. I'm coming, tiggers."

But when he saw Pooh, Piglet, Rabbit, Roo, and Eeyore, Tigger stopped short. "What are you guyses doing here?" he asked.

"We came to look for you," Rabbit snapped. "It's not safe out here."

"I'm not going home," Tigger shouted. "I'm waiting here for my REAL FAMILY." His voice echoed through the woods and over the hills.

Seconds later, a huge rumbling

sound thundered through the forest. And a wall of snow came crashing down the hill. It was an avalanche, and it was coming straight for Tigger and his friends!

"Quick—into the tree!" Tigger shouted, bouncing his friends up into the safety of the branches. But just as he was about to crawl up himself, the snow swept him off his feet and carried him toward the edge of a steep cliff.

"Oh no! Oh no! Oh d-dear!" cried Rabbit and Piglet.

Suddenly Roo knew what to do. "The Whoop-de-Dooper Loop-de-

Looper Alley-Ooper Bounce!" he shouted. He wound up, and leaped into the air. Bouncing across the snow, he grabbed Tigger's tail and pulled him to safety, just in time!

chapter

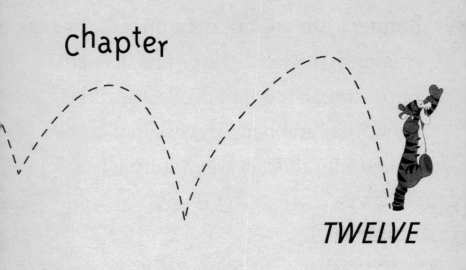

TWELVE

At last the avalanche passed. Everyone climbed down from the tree and gathered around. "A magnificent job! Very well done! Bravo!" they shouted to Roo.

Tigger beamed with pride and

slapped Roo on the back. "What a Whoop-de-Doopin' Loop-de-Loopin' Alley-Oopin' Bounce that was!"

On their way back home, they ran into Christopher Robin.

"Where have you all been?" asked Christopher Robin.

"We were looking for Tigger looking for Tigger's family," explained Pooh.

"Tigger's . . . family?" asked Christopher Robin. "You didn't have to go looking for them!" he said.

"But . . . but I got their letter! And it said . . ." Tigger searched for his letter, but couldn't find it. "I guess I lost it in the avallyanche," he cried. "And now, I can't even remember the words."

"Dear Tigger, just a note to say . . ." started Owl.

"Dress warmly," said Kanga.

"Eat well," said Pooh.

"Stay safe and sound," said Piglet.

"Keep smiling," said Eeyore.

"We're always there for you," said Roo.

"Signed, Your Family."

Tigger looked around at his friends. He was beginning to understand. "You mean . . . you fellows are my family?" he asked.

"I'm afraid we have nothing better to offer," said Pooh.

"Well, of course not, Pooh Boy. 'Cause there's nothing better than the best! And, I should have seen it all along!" said Tigger.

The next day, Tigger threw a family reunion in his house, complete with presents for everyone. Piglet got lots of firewood. Pooh got enough honey to last the winter. And Tigger gave Eeyore his brand-new family room addition. Tigger saved the best present of all for Roo—the shiny, heart-shaped locket with a picture of all the Hundred-Acre friends inside—a true family portrait indeed.